W9-CPE-631

Having created Heaven and Earth, flowers, creatures, and humankind, the gods created happiness. But where should happiness be? In the deepest abyss, in the most luminous star, in the darkest cave?

After long reflection, the wisest, most ancient god decided: "We will hide happiness in the very heart of human beings. There they will find it.....if they look."

—An Eastern Tale

One a day reason to be Happy

Laura Archera Huxley

Illustrated by Mimi Stuart

CompCare Publications
2415 Annapolis Lane, Minneapolis, MN 55441

©1986 Laura Archera Huxley

All rights reserved
Published in the United States
by CompCare Publications,
a division of Comprehensive Care Corporation

Reproduction in whole or part, in any form, including storage
in memory device systems, is forbidden without written permission
. . . except that portions may be used in broadcast or printed
commentary or review when attributed fully to author and
publication by names.

Library of Congress Cataloging-in-Publication Data

Huxley, Laura Archera.
   Oneadayreason to be happy.

   Summary: A dolphin encourages people to share the
little things that happen each day that make them happy.
   [1. Happiness—Fiction] I. Title. II. Title: One
a day reason to be happy.
PZ7.H96740n 1986   [Fic]   86-21632
ISBN 0-89638-112-9
ISBN 0-89638-111-0 (pbk.)

Type design by Susan Rinek
Illustrations by Mimi Stuart

Inquiries, orders, and catalog requests should be addressed to
CompCare Publications
2415 Annapolis Lane
Minneapolis, Minnesota 55441
Call toll-free 800/328-3330
(Minnesota residents 612/559-4800)

To Karen
my eleven-year-old granddaughter who, after reading
these pages, added with the lightning speed of timelessness
the last line: the essential message of the book.

My deepest thanks...

to my friend and agent Dorris Halsey, who with her quick
intuition and her concern for others, caught a wandering
idea and nurtured it into a book;

to my editor Bonnie Hesse for her skill in gracefully
navigating this book through the mysterious waters of
the publishing world;

to the memory of Antonietta Lilly, who loved Abraxas
and might be celebrating with him now — in The High Sea;

and to my family, genetic and extended, near and far,
gratefulness and love for its support without bounds.

When are you brighter, more generous, more supportive to yourself and others: when you are well and happy — or when you are unwell and unhappy? Your answer to these questions is the reason for this book.

Most of us, when well and happy, are willing and capable of understanding and cheerfulness. Conversely, how can we exude empathic feelings when in the grip of physical or mental pain? Can I think of others when I suffer an excruciating earache? Or when my dearest one is desperately ill?

In the prodigious catalogues of Learning Centers for all ages, there are tempting courses for achieving security and success. What about training and discovering, within and without, *oneadayreason* for happiness?

From kindergarten on, children trained to bring their teacher, as daily homework, one reason to be happy, will have a better day in school and, as such awareness becomes second nature, it will beneficially influence all their lives.

For us grownups, focusing on present reasons for happiness might prevent us from blindly destroying them: might remind us to give "equal time" to good news.

Folk wisdom has always known the decisive influence of happiness and humor in staying well and getting well. Now medical science has given official sanction to the healing power of good mood.

Total happiness is a rare gift, said the French writer Colette. But little happinesses are available.

Encouraged by Abraxas, a dolphin whose name means "darkness disappear," let us find and accept free-floating gifts of little happinesses and, at times, luminous offerings of good will, beauty, and love.

Laura Huxley

Come—I will show you
how to swim underwater.

Did you see? Did you see down there?
I saw a big thing.

That big thing is a dolphin!
He is trapped in the net!
He will die if we don't free him —
he must come up to breathe.
Let's save him!

You made me free!

Let's celebrate!

Come ride on me.

You saved my life! What can I do for you?

I want
a motorbike.

I want
big earrings.

Yes, yes — you will get those things.
But listen: you are so young, I am so old.
I am thirty million years old.
I can teach you something new!

Thirty million years old!
You are older than Grandfather!

Yes. Older than your grandfather and your great-great-great-grandfather. What would you like to learn?

To play baseball? To ride a horse? Wait, we know! Everybody wants to learn how to be happy!

Yes, everybody!
Go and come back
with people from
everywhere.

Tell them that I am
one of the ancient
people of the sea.

My name is
Abhadda-Kedabrah.
Call me Abraxas
for short.

Come! Abraxas, the talking dolphin,
will tell us how to be happy.

How did you learn to ride a bike?

By riding a bike!

How did you learn to teach?

By teaching!

How is your child learning to walk?

By walking!

How did you learn to play the trumpet?

By playing the trumpet!

How are we going to find *oneadayreason* to be happy?

By finding it!

Hurray! Tomorrow and tomorrow and tomorrow
I will be waiting for you to tell me your
oneadayreason to be happy.

Last night my husband and I
had the same dream at the same time!

My rat, Bellezza, was sick and
now she is well again!

I am happy because I did everything by myself today.

I am happy
because I found
a blue feather.

Today
my time is
all mine!

I was so afraid to ask for a job — but I asked.

My little boy worked all his playtime
to make me just the present I wanted.

Look what I found today!

I fixed this old car. Nobody wanted it
because it couldn't work and now it works!

I am happy because last night my Daddy read me a story while I was going to sleep.

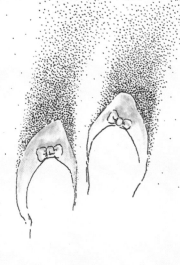

I could not walk. Then every night I saw
myself walking and every day I took
a small, small, small step and now I walk!

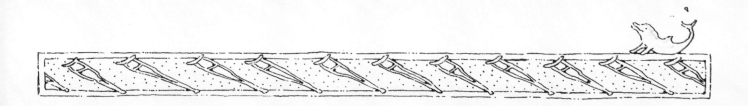

I am happy because I was so angry at my
little brother but I did not hit him.

I can imagine anything I want.

I heard people speaking about beauty,
about tree branches dancing in the wind.
I thought it was all nonsense,
that they were putting on airs.
But today I am so happy because
I understood, in a flash, the beauty
of trees and leaves and flowers!
Now I can feel how beautiful beauty is!

I am happy because I saved a bee —
and it did not sting me this time.

I am happy because Mommy let me
help my little sister with her shoes.

I am happy because I have no pain today!

I am happy because nobody shouted at home today.

I was
dreaming of
angels kissing my face.
When I woke up the
dream continued—
the angels were
raindrops.

I am happy because I was frightened
and my father did not laugh at me.

Yesterday was a noisy, hectic day, but at night I found a silent, secure place between two stars.

She is not
scratching.

He is not
biting me.

I am happy because
Mommy and Daddy
smiled at each other.

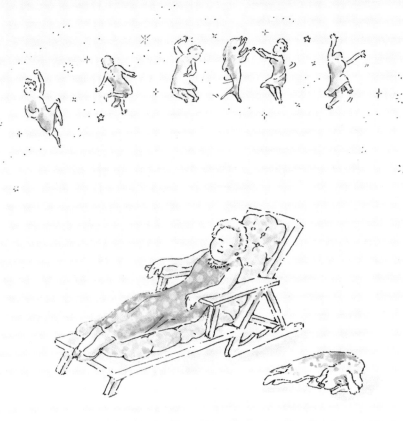

I can no longer walk,
but I can still dream and dance inside.

I am happy because
the flower spoke to me only.

I thought I was a coward because
I was afraid of heights. Now I know
I am not a coward because I was so afraid,
but I climbed that dangerous peak.

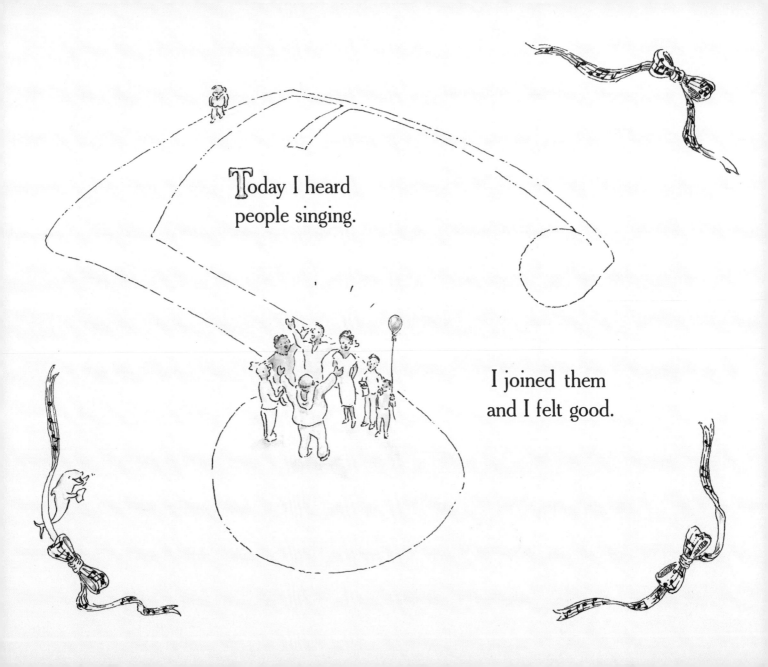

Today I heard
people singing.

I joined them
and I felt good.

I am happy because my big sister
did not say that I was too young.

I am happy because I had a scary dream,
but I woke up and it was not true.

Today I understood what real giving is:
I saw my child give away his favorite toy.
It was all *his* idea, not mine.

I am happy because my Mommy
is not going to work today.

I was angry with my mother-in-law.
I told her so and she took me out
to the happiest lunch I ever had!

I am happy because the children
did not make fun of me today.

My wife knew I lost my job.
She didn't say anything
but prepared my
favorite dish,
quietly.

 am happy because last night the moon was all mine.

I am happy because I got
in the bubble bath with Mommy.

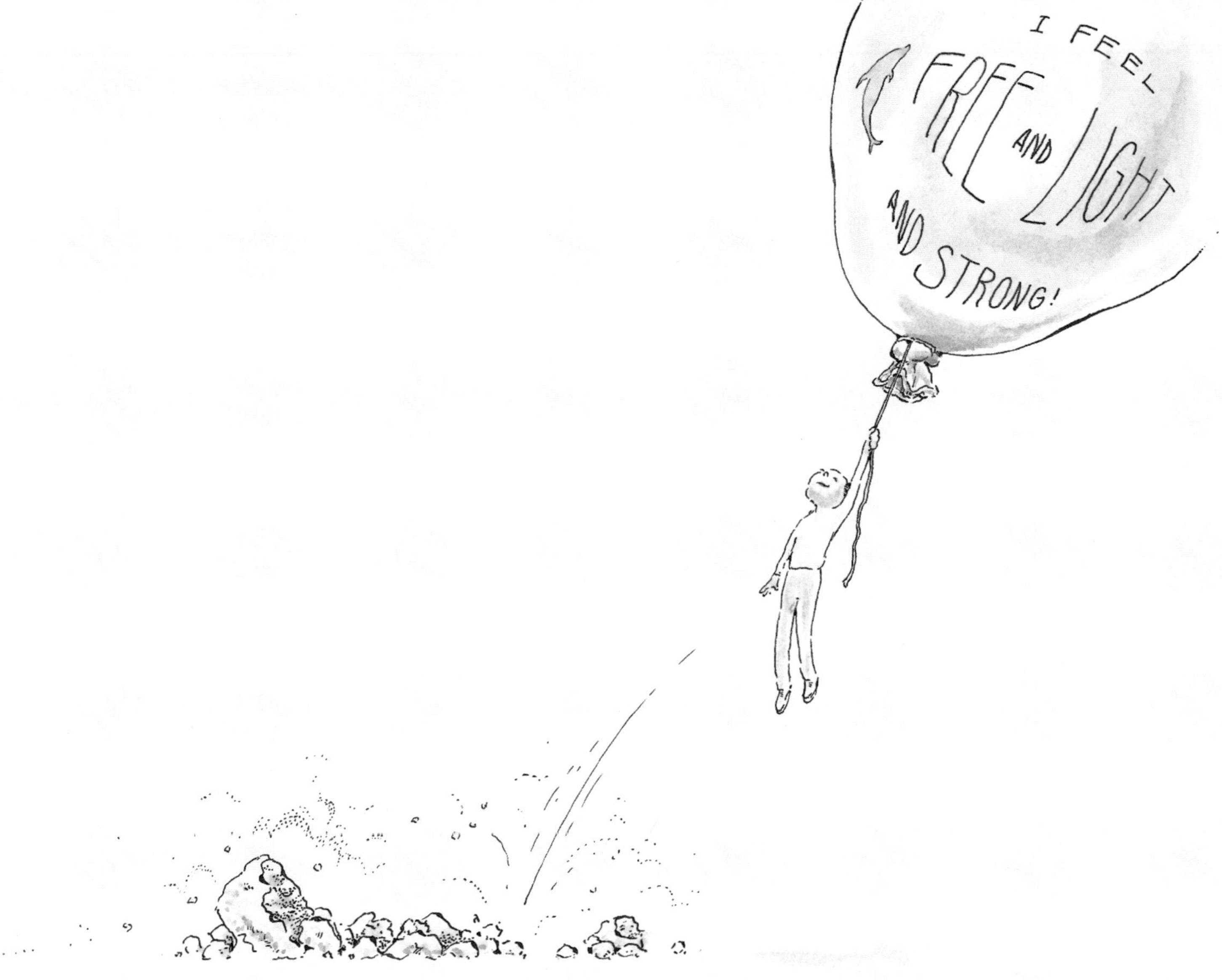
I FEEL
FREE AND LIGHT
AND STRONG!

Everybody
told me
I couldn't do it,
but I can!

We are happy because
we found this poem!

Night
and
day
in
every
way
we are
becoming
better
and
better

Night and day in every way

We are happy because
we put music to the poem and sing it!

We are happy because
we dance the poem all together!

we are becoming better and better

NIGHT AND
DAY IN EVERY WAY
WE ARE BECOMING BETTER AND BETTER

I am happy because
when I go to sleep
I write the poem on the sky!
Every night I change the
colors of the letters!

Karen, what makes your eyes so bright?
Tell me your oneadayreason to be happy
and I will tell the whole world!

I am happy because

I AM !